Silvia Cecchini

BACH FLOWERS' FAIRY TALES

INDEX

Chicory.............................. 6
Mimulus........................... 13
Agrimony......................... 20
Scleranthus...................... 28
Clematis.......................... 35
Centaury......................... 42
Gentian........................... 50
Vervain........................... 58
Cerato............................. 65
Impatiens........................ 73
Rock Rose....................... 80
Water Violet.................... 88

Come with me, take my hand and fly with me over the gates of this city park....
Near the big yew-tree, you'll beleive to see many little lights. You could think they are fireflies, or reflections of starlight on the wet grass, but take an advice: close your eyes, thus your heart will be able to hear Fairy Violet's sweet voice, who speaks to a little people...

"My little ones, each of you, finally grown up, has now got the time to fly up out of here. You are the little people of the flowers, but what you do not yet know is that, among the flowers, there are some really special ones. They were called, by a clever human being, the Twelve Healers. A virtue belongs to each of Them, or, better, each of them belongs to a Virtue.
These flowers need a special care, need to be protected and looked after.Each of you, deva or fairy, will choose which one to take care of. Thus, attending your flower, you'll get the chance to evolve and to help humans, spirits of nature, every being of the Universe. To help you in the choice of the flower to which devote your service, I'll tell you twelve stories.

These are tales of flowers and litlle humans. Even if the human race so many times opposed to us, spoiling our mother earth, we decided to consider that people as our brothers, since so much need our help.
Let's begin with the story of a very common flower: chicory...."

CHICORY

" The old Romans honoured the goddess Ceres, Mother Earth " the teacher is telling " who was also named Demeter, or Gaia…"
"Like me! She's called like me! " Gaia shouts from her seat, rousing the knitting of the teacher's brows.
"The Goddess' symbol is the ear of wheat, since wheat is our nourishment, and, like the earth, gives its whole plant to feed us human and animals…"
"I like very much the cuscus cooked by my aunt, it's made with the wheat!"
Again, the teacher stares at Gaia, severely, and proceeds: - As the Earth continuously nurtures all her inhabitants, so Ceres, become mother, deeply loved her daughter Persefone…but I'll tell you this story another time…Today, since we talked about wheat, I want to accompany you outside, in the near countryside, where there is a beautiful cornfield …"
The teacher controls that everyone, really everyone, is fastening the sweater, and that everyone has gone to pee. Gaia really does not

stand her when she behaves in such a way: as if they were not able to manage on their own! Moreover, she always objects to their hair, which ought to be tied, and to their nails, which ought to be shorter, and to their socks which ought to be pulled up....Could she think about her own socks, instead, with that evident ladder!

"Gaia, could you borrow me your pencils , today, if you do not use them?" Here comes Irene who, as usual, bores her with her mournful voice.

"No, the pencils are mine, you better had to think to carry yours, today!" Well said! Gaia says to herself: now, perhaps, Irene shall learn the lesson....

While the class is walking on the path towards the cornfield, Gaia looks among the bushes, along the ditch. She can see things that others cannot. Some time ago she realized this fact, since when she told Mom she had a fairy, and also a smorf. She saw in Mom's eyes that quiet incredulity reserved to a daydreaming child. Ma she was not daydreaming. Neither she does now, as she sees two little beings running away behind a bramble, Just in time to escape from her friends. *Devas*, her aunt said. Her aunt is a kind of wizard, she once heard Dad saying so, therefore Gaia took courage and told her of the little beings she could see, sometimes, in the wood or in the countryside, near trees, bushes, flowers. They are *devas*, and they are somehow the flowers' guardians, as Maria, in her school, who cleans the toilet and sells the sandwiches. For this reason, Gaia is not surprised at all when she sees a blue little spirit, with blue eyes and a slim body, so quick that she scarsely suceeds in seeing his contours during his fast movements. He is waiting for her, sitting under his plant, athe edge of the cornfield.

The teacher has begun speaking of the wheat and gets into the field, with the class, while Gaia stops near this blue flowered plant, *chicory*, as the teacher called it .

"Look at me" the plant says "look at the marvel of my flowers. There is nothing else deserving your attention, hereby."

The plant's deva grumbles, and, without even showing to have noticed Gaia, turns to the plant: "If only once you tried to leave your flowers open after noon, when the sun shines

high in the sky, you'ld feel a great joy in feeling your petals lightened by his rays...."
"By whom? By that bighead? Not on my life, I prefer to close them so I won't see the airs he's giveng himself....but don't distract me, now, tiresome...let me talk with my public..."
Gaia looks around a couple of times, and eventually she realizes that Chicory is addressing to her. So, she gets nearer. With her fingers touches the flower's petals and then, yes, she does not resist, also the little spirit who is sitting on the flower, looking cross.
" I thouhgt that plants liked the sun; the teacher says that the flowers follow the sun in its revolution, during the day..."
"Ah , my dear!" Chicory answers to her " but those kind of plants have no backbone, being so ready to kneel in front of His Majesty...The sun, at the beginning of the day, still is a acceptable and discreet neighbor, but after a while he becomes more and more intrusive and he steals the public attention , he always wants to be at the center of the stage!...."
Gaia, thoughtful, says. " You know, Chicory, we, Dad and my sister, always sing a song which says "to get a tree, you need a flower..."

"True, true!" Chicory nods.
"To get a flower, you need the ground..."
"Well, I don't know if it's really so..." Chicory shakes her petals, uneasy.
"To get the ground, you need the sun: to get a flower, you need the sun...."
"Ah no!" And Chicory turns away, offended, while the blue spirit is happily fluttering beating his wings as if applauding Gaia's words.
Now Gaia tries to put it right: " Besides, I think we could also say that...Apollo, you know, is the God of the sun, and the old Romas told that every morning he carried it whit his cart to let him lighten the hearth.....In short, if Apollo knew that there are no flowers to be lighted by the sun, I thought he would not tire to carry out the sun (at least, Dad does so, on Sunday...he lets the car in the garage all day long, since he does not carry us to school)...therefore, " Gaia concludes, with satisfaction " the sun, to rise in the sky, needs to know that some flower waits for him....the sun needs flowers!"
"Yes, oh yes!" Chicory and the deva shout together, beating leaves and wings...

"Perhaps, today, only for today, I'm doing it just for you, and I hope you'll thank me for this.." Chicoy says to the deva "I'll open my petals also after noon..."
Gaia looks at her watch and sees that actually noon is past by ten minutes; in fact the teacher is coming back with the class. The sun shines on the blue petals, making them even more blue...but, how strange, some little drops appear, on the corolla of the Chicory flower.
"What happens?" Gaia asks to the deva. And he, smiling : "It happens that she did not remember this" And he puts on his sunglasses " now she weeps because of too much light... "
Smiling, Gaia picks up some drops with her fingers , then suck them, while the teacher is explaining: "The chicory flowers open only from sunrise to noon, therefore now you can not see them ..It is a pity because their blue is beautiful and would be well portraied in your pictures and photos...." But the teachers stops in the middle of the sentence, amazed of that beautiful chicory plant, with her widely open flowers, not caring of the light.
"Strange" she says. She picks up a flower and put it in her hair, knowing that it will recall the

blue of her eyes. A drop falls from the flower to her face, and the teacher licks it away.

Gaia has just said good bye to the deva, who is hidding himself in the cornfield, when she suddenly feels her heart opening like the Chicory flowers. She then feels the wish to go near Irene, and to offer her a blue pencil, so that she'll be able to complete her picture.

"Gaia, don't you make any pictures? "The teacher begins blaming her, but after a while she stops, smiling within herself, she hugs, saying: "It does not matter... Boys, girls, half an hour of free play! Go wild, if you do not kill yourself is enough!"

Laughing, the teacher lays down on the grass, and she does not notice that the deva is playing with the flower in her hair....

"Therefore, the chicory learned the beauty of sharing her life with others, learned that she did not possessed any individual life, since each of us is nothing without the others. To get a flower, you need a seed; to get a seed, you need a fruit ....Chicory learned the beauty of unconditioned love, of sacrifice. Her deva will pour this virtue in each single drop of blue used to colour her petals...."

Now, half-open your eyes...Don't you see some lights, becoming blue, and flying away? Don't you hear the sound of whispered good-byes?....oh, no more now...That lasted only for a twinkling of an eye, because Fairy Violet thas begun another tale...

MIMULUS

Mimma is going back home, from the Music school orchestra rehearsal. While holding the violin with her right hand , she is still wiping some tears of humiliation.
Dario and all the boys of the wind section have gone on all the afternoon in scaring her, only to laugh after her. First, they hidden themselves behind the main door, then in the girls' toilets, and, when she did not expect it, they jumped out playing cymbals or blowing trumpets in her ears, scaring her to death, and making her to jump out and cry. Moreover, during the rehearsal, Dario came behind her, and it seemed that he deliberately was playing cymbals near her head.... often her violin palyed false notes, and the teacher blamed her. Her heart beated violently up and down, continuously, and her stomach was nearly getting out of her mouth....Still now, while she leaves the main road to walk on the path through the field, she still feels that feeling of fear, she is afraid of any lizard which could creep along her feet, or of.....HERE IT IS! A scream comes out of her mouth, as she sees,

just in front of herself, a little mouse slipping away through the grass...The scream has scared it , even more than her, and it has jumped on, has changed direeCtion and has run away....

Still trembling (but perhaps she has never stopped , since she began trembling together with Dario's cymbals), Mimma sits upon a rock, just for a while, the violin case put on the pebbles, near the stream carrying water from the mountains to the city.

To sit quietly just for a while, only few steps from the main road, but near grass and pebbles, gives her some peace, in the silence. No cars, no people, only running water. She often feels the sensation to be in three: she, the world around her, and somebody, hidden beyond the corner, waiting the right moment to shake her . Now, on the contrary, she feels well, all alone: she, and the world. And with...those beautiful yellow flowers, born there, in equilibrium, among the pebbles of river bank. "You, beautiful flower" Mimma says "I would like to be like you...here you are, among dangers, in a moment your roots could come away, your seeds could fall in the water, the wind could carry you with him..yet you are happy anyway, smiling with your red spots on your yellow petals, and you compete with the water for laughing more....And, while her hand touches lightly the plant which she's chattering with, Mimma feels the impulse to catch a flower , to carry it with her.

She does not care of the mouse, which, still scared , slips behind her, towards the rich traesures of the dust-bins forward, near the side-walk. Now the sky is all covered by huge grey clouds, a summer storm is brewing, a big one with lightenings and thunders that scare Mimma so much, and make her to be always teased by her brother. Here is the first thunder, far away: it's only a rumble... wish it does not come nearer..Mimma hurries up. The first drops fall down: tic, tac, toc, tic....some drops sprinkle the flowers' petals, and Mimma wipe them off with her hand, protective. Here comes another thunder, and at once her hand springs to her ears, to cover it, then...her thumb in her mouth, as when she was a baby... The taste of the floweris still on the thumb....a yelllow taste, of sun and wet grass....Now a lightening dispells the clouds, but...how strange , Mimma is no more afraid, on the contrary she thinks that u there the light engineer has a very good time...now, maybe, the sound of the cymbales also will arrivecome, the sound of that fantastic orchestra which is hidden beyond the clouds....And, in fact, there comes a GONG much louder than Dario's cymbals.....Wonderful! Such a wish to play! Laughing, Mimma opens the violin case, and , playing and walking, with the flower in her mouth, and rain drops rebounded against the violin, on the flower, and from the flower on her face, on her lips, she wishes to dance more and more, and to jump, under that summer storm, which once would have shaken her and made her to hid under the blankets, covering her ears. The rain is now falling better and better, and washes the flower.Drops slip down, to the ground, in the drain pipe of the pavement, where, hidden near the entrance of the drain, the litlle mouse is sipping some water. Water of flower, of yellowness and sun, of wet grass, of joy and will to risk..the mouse, drunk with this water, gets into the drain, towards the usual underworld dangers. But this time things are different, it feels inside itself a new energy, the never felt before audacity of an explorer ...Just arrived at the back of one of those common underworld smorf, instead of hiddening itself, he cries, with all the air of its small lungs. A defeaning SQUEEK causes the smorf to start and to dash out. Up, up, out of the gully-hole, just in the draian-pipe.

The smorf recovers from the shock, and begins to appreciate that splendid grey weather, drainy and muddy, those fine lightenings and thunders so scaring for some people (and for this reason so regenerating for itself), but...it realizes that it feels weaker and weaker, just as it were melting. How come? Usually it is the sun which has this kind of effect on its race...but there is not even a pale ray...only a coat of clouds who renders the city gloomier than ever....why then this sense of stupid joy, where does this light come from, this light which devoures, which dissolves?

And just a moment before its consciousness vanishes, liquefied, inthe gully-hole, with the rain, then it realizes. It is able to realize the origin of all that light: it is a small yellow petal, just near the puddle...

"Oh, yes...What a great lesson can give us that flower...the courage to live a common life, among people whom we can like or dislike, but with whom we'll behave with compassion and pity...
Sometimes our compassion will be a helpin hand, sometimes it will be a cutting sword...The yellow mimulus liquefied the smorf, and the death of that smorf was the birth of a new being....Nothing is destroyed, everything is transformed...
When you need , take the courage to use the sword, but do it always with compassion...
But, perhaps do you think that it is better always to shake hands, and to show a smiling face? Well, then you ought to listen to the next story...."

AGRIMONY

"Armando, little Armando..." Mom is calling him from a distance "come for a snack!...."
"Little Arm-ando!.....BIG ARM! Go and take your chocolate-infant-bottle, go!...." His friends run after him.
Armando is rithmically jumping while he goes away, loughing, and says:" Look me rolling away...a real fat lump rolling towards its afternoon feast..." He laughs again, turning back sometime to control if his improvised sketch caused the hoped laughters.
There is only one moment when Armando's face becomes serious, maybe sad, but it is only a moment, and at once passes, as soon as he comes into the kitchen and finds bread and chocolate waiting for him, and the last number of his favourite comic bought by Mom. Then, with his trophies, goes directly to sprawl in front of TV, waiting for dinner....and for after dinner, with nuts or popcorn.
Fairy Wilhelmine, like every other evening when it becomes dark, has just told good bye to her plant, and is going to explore the neighborhood. *Her* plant, she thinks. Her

Agrimony, Saint William's plant, has just flowered. So humble to grow out of the gardens, near the edges of the ditches, but so right, so erect upon the grass around her, like she were a steeple of a cathedral , her yellow flowers bringing joy, and the moral rightness which connect them directly to heaven , not allowing any lye. Every time she flowers it is like a miracle, and a new strenght pushes Wilhelmina to bring her message to all who need it. Here, for example, beyond this half-closed window, there is this fat boy, Armando. She has benn observing him since some time ago, and she has been watching his night meals with chocolate cups and cakes, while watching the TV in front his bed, looking at false scenes of a false world, where everyone is beautiful, with false smiles and false tears. Armando, she thinks, learned from there. He learned to pretend. To pretend also with himself that everything is OK, always. He learned to change the subject, when he feels that some tears could appear, and he does that with ease, as he changed the TV channel by the remote control. Tonight the fairy really wishes to chatter with him. And Wilhelmina goes into the room, just in the middle of Armando sipping a hot chocolate cup. The cup is readily posed on the bed-side table, not to pour even a drop of it, by a completely astonished Armando. "What? A Flower fairy.....Fianlly, little Rose sometimes is right about her fancies...and what are you doing here? Would you like some chocolate?"

"No, thanks, chocolate makes me fatten, and then I would have some problem to fly...I want to mantain my shape, not like you......"

"But me" Armando says " I *want* to be fat, I do it on purpose.."

"Do you really think that I swallow this? Me not, sure, not today that I am so full of the sincerity transmitted from my plant, not today when I recognize lies from miles away....Now tell me the real reason why you wish to remain fat!" And the fairy, saying this, sprinkles on him some fairy's dust.

"I..."Armando mumbles, under the effect of the fairy dust, which makes him sincere, "I...want to remain fat 'cause I don't want to stay alone...'cause I make my friend laugh of me...I play the fool...and so they let me play with them...."

"So do you think" Fairy Wilhelmina, now, is shaking before Armando's nose her magic wand " that you are not able to amuse somenone unless you're fat? Look at yourself in the mirror..."

Armando now looks at his image into the mirror wardrobe, suddenly becoming slim, his pajama hanging in every direction. This, besides his bewildered look, makes fairy Wilhelmina burst into laughter... She laughs, laughs.... while Armando touches himself and finds out that he is still fat, that it is the mirror which makes him see himself slim...She laughs, and laughs rolling in the air and making somersaults...while Armando begins pulling faces at the mirror, to try his new look...she loughs keeing her hands on her belly under the short yellow shirt, and her flight becomes dizzy, making her skim over the chocolate cup. "Go away from my chocolate" Armando snarls, pretending to be angry, and from Wilhelmina, who is tearing because of the laughter, two great tearss fall down into the cup, while she flies away. Armando, now, still sneering but sulky for the fairy's trick, drinks the chocolate, using the same old habit of changing channel when something disturbs him. So, the Agrimony's sincerity enters deeply into him, much sweeter than the chocolate.

Armando looks at himself at the mirror, and sees again that slim Armando, his joyful face a little more adult, guessed under the full moon features. Honestly, he realizes that he would like to try a slim look, to feel light and to be able to play better, without hearing friends calling him "Big ball....human bomb.... " He realizes too that he is afraid not to succeed, and that he will need help. One, two sobs move his belly, and eventually, after the sobs, real tears spread on his face.

He put himself under the blankets, strangely in peace in spite of his tears, and Fairy Wilhelmina's wings caress his face , before flying out of the window.

In this season the weather is very hot and Armando and his friends found a shelter in the cool Mary's house, in front of the park. " Go on, Armando, let us laugh , and then we'll give you a cake, go on!..." The boys begin teasing him, as usual. But today Armando looks like a new boy: he feels secure, upright, growing towards the sky like a pinnacle, and looks right in his friends'eyes, telling them, sincerely: " Boys... Now I feel really bad. I understood that I do not like to be fat, and I don't want to laugh, or make you laugh, either...and if you prefer me to go home, tell it....it is impossible that things go worst ..." But the eyes which look at him are open, good, curious of this new Armando that they see, and his friends, one by one, begin to say " Well, let be us that make you smile", "It's me that will tell you a joke..." " I want to tell you how my mother made us eat vegetable soup for one month, because she was on diet, and eventually she became slim, and she became friendlier, too.." "And I promise that I shall no more offer to you icecream"..." What? Did you ever offered to me anything?, you, great stingy boy, you hardly offer something to yourself!!". Finally, with laughter and pats on his shoulders, Armando regains his good humour, and Mary's grandma comes near, saying to Piercarlo to stop eating chips or he won't have dinner. And she knits her brows, to make him understand that it is not good to eat such things in front of Armando, in order not to provoke him. Armando catches the point and says, on impulse "Ok, out the garbage, or better, I do you want to know what I'll do? Since today, I'll be on diet. It willbe hard, but I'll succeed ". He gets out of his rugsack his chocolate snack and gives it to Rose, Rocco's little sister, who is lamenting she is hungry.

With her mouth full of chocolate, Rose jumps on Armando's back, throwing her arms around his neck, and whispering " I love you, Nanno....."

As soon as it is dark, Fairy Wilhelmina flies before the windows of Armando's house. She sees Armando, sitting at the table and talking to his mother. Mom is listening to him, seriously. Then, she smiles, nodding, embraces him, and put in the fridge the cake she had just taken out. At the TV, the usual plastic-face entertainer is showing his teeth, pretending to smile. Armando looks at the TV and makes a grimace. He catches the remote control and, just before he switches TV off, Wilhelmina sees, beyond the plastic face, something real in the entertainer's eyes, something special, something....." Well, for tonight I've finished, but maybe tomorrow night I'll go to visit him , too..." And, with a beat of the wing, she goes on doing the neighborhood rounds...

"For some days, no more sweets for the fat boy...In a while, he'll learn to show his feelings, he'll learn not to escape from real life into any kind of excess. Since Agrimony belongs to Temperance, the right mean between extremes, her fairy shall dance among her leaves and flowers, bringing peace in lights and shadows, in laughters and tears...
Good-bye, newborn fairies, take care of saint William's plant...."

What happens? A whir of fairy wings, some sparkling lights dance near the yew, then disappear in the starry night.
Perhaps you feel some drops on your skin, perhaps you would like to taste if they are salty tears, but, please, make attention, and listen again to Fairy Violet....

SCLERANTHUS

Daisy hugs Flake, her little home rabbit, while she accompanies her towards freedom. Daisy's mother and father decided to divorce: they'll live in two different towns, in city houses, and she shall no more be allowed to keep Flake, who used to stay in the garden. Mom and Dad carried her to this field, which, they knew, is the ideal spot for rabbits, since there are plenty of burrows and wild rabbits. Flake, as soon as has been put on the ground, explores, shy, while Daisy sits aside. She said that she will not come back to the car until she'll be sure that Flake gets well. Therefore, she sits down, taking her time, and waits. Also for her this moment is very important . She has been told that she's now grown enough to choose if to live with Dad or with Mummy. Sure, she'll see both, anyway: but one of them only during the summer, the other one will stay with her during the school year. In the past days, she cried a lot, but ther was nothing to do: not any other chance, they told her. Therefore, now she has to choose. Her sight goes by chance to a daisy:

who knows if that flower, whose name is hers too, will help her to choose. Thus, she begins in picking up the petals: Dad, Mom, Dad, Mom....but, while she's pulling out one petal after another, she seems to tear away bits of her own heart, the things she'll going to miss. Going to miss Dad reading to her stories, in the evening, or Mummy's hands combing her hair....Soon, the daisy, not yet finished, falls down on the ground, while Daisy shakes her head, crying a little.

Over there, not far, Flake has met a little grey rabbit, which seems to invite her to follow him, but she stops, turns back, watch her, then comes back. Then, when she is half way, again she stops, moves her nose, turns back, and goes again towards the rabbit. This happens a couple of times, until eventually she stops just in the middle of the field, still like a statue.

Days lies down with her belly on the grass, and her look goes to a strange plant in front of her. which she did not notice before, so insignificant it is. What a strange flowers, without petals! Or, better, with petals that look like leaves... is it a flower, that one? But , as if it were answering to her question, she hears a voice talking inside her head: *"Of course it is a flower, it is my flower...I am the spirit of Scleranthus, and, if you like, I 'll tell you the story of my plant, which, long time ago, had to face a difficult decision...I could call it* The story of the non- choice...*"*

Daisy, who is too excited to say something, nods thinking "sure, sure I like to hear, especially now that I do not know what to choose...."

"When my first ancestor was going to flower, for the first time on this planet, Mother earth told her to decide the colour of her petals, choosing between pink and yellow. The days and the nights passed and the small plant, overwhelmed by that responsibility, as soon as was going to choose yellow , then began thinking to all the love she couldexpress if her flowers were pink; while, if she was going to decide for e pink, suddenly she complained not to wear the joy of the yellow . Therefore, as the moment of the flowering came, she had not yet decided, and the last night Mother Nature, moved to compassion , gave her the gift of imagination. Thus, we scleranthus can , today, imagine the petals we like more, coloured in

any way, and we are happy, as a white light ray which, passing through a prism, projects on the wall the colours of a whole rainbow...."

What a beautiful story, Daisy thinks, and what a pity that she cannot ask Mother Nature the same gift! Other tears fall from her eyes just onto the plant's flowers.

Here comes Flake, still uncertain if to stay or to go. She moves her nose towards the plant, amazed of those mixed smells: the scleranthus scents and the smell of Daisy's tears, which she has already met , when, in the last days, she was comforting her.

Flake chews one scleranthus flower, become curious of the odd mixture.

Flake, now, sees things with different eyes. There is a new world, in front of her, so open, so full of adventures! And the burrow which that grey rabbit has gone into seems to invite her to explore.

She looks at Daisy, seeing a girl who is giving her all that freedom. The love who accompanies this gift will stay forever with Flake, and will come back to Daisy, multiplied, to make her happy in turn.

Flake decides to go, now, but first she brings her little snout near Daisy's face, still sad; like she did last days so many times, she gives her some licks, mixed with the flower juice she is still chewing. Then, after receiving her tender pats, she happily jumps far away, towards her new life.

Daisy looks at the white flake ,which is her rabbit's tale, disappearing into a burrow, and she feels strange. She is somehow sorry not to stay with Flake anymore, but at the same time she is happy her friend found a new family....Then, all these mixed feelings of joy and sadness are overcome by a wave of confidence, which widen her hearth and her belly. Now, it is as if she knew that for herself too there is a new life full of beautiful and unexpected things, and that, any were the choice she makes, everything will go better and better. She takes another daisy and begins picking its petals: with Mummy (and inside her head ideas form about lazy breakfasts, and make-ups in front of the mirror, and a tender and perfumed body hugging her....); with Daddy (and here comes ideas of wind in the hair while bycicling and talking, and popcorn at the movies, and battles of tickling ..); and so on, petal after petal, good things add to good things, and colours to colours, like for the small plant who was not able to choose....

"Got the point? There is an old book, written by human sages, which says:

*Each person has her own path.
Every path belongs to God.
Each step of the path, as well as
the footstep itself, belongs to God.
Even the shadow of the foot
belongs to God.
All paths lead to God.*

Each street is a wonderflul one; only the virtue of Constance will reveal its beauty, sooner or later....And the beauty is really everywhere, no need to fly high to discover it: listen to the next story..."

CLEMATIS

Caroline is sitting at her desk, ready to begin the housework of geometric design: a project of a city park. The teacher, knowing that she and the rest of the class, so *artists,* so *creative*, as he ironically addresses them, do not stand geometry and definite perspectives, decided to make a gift to the class and assigned this unusual homework.
Outside, in the sunny afternoon, a white butterfly has stopped on a branch of a tree and now looks down, down, at the flowers waiting for her to be helped to exchange their love messages. But she, up there, stays so well, so high, so far from the boring life of a butterfly....
A city park, Caroline thinks, looking at the white sheet where a line has just been traced. Her eyes go up, seeing a lake, streams, statues, and fountains, and boats under the willows...when she look down again, oh , mine....! The drawing paper is all doodled with flowers, sketches of dreaming girls, and couples feeding the swans....There is nothing

geometric, she suddenly realizes. Thus, she takes another sheet...

Outside, Chleo, the butterfly, is dancing valzer among the flowers. She wanders about aimlessly, she enjoys the fresh air and flies higher and higher, towards the clouds, dreaming of far places, and of the sea, and , beyond the sea, of coloured countries scented by spices....

Caroline, after the first two straight lines, has already changed her picture in oriental pagodeas, and indonesian temples, Buddha statues, and a watermill, and why not a windmill....She observes the sheet, now all covered of sketches, and in her ears the teacher's voice resound: "Remember, all of you, no Disneyland!....."

"Help!...I'll do another attempt" Caroline thinks, as she switches the music on, going to dance a valzer, she too....

Now Chleo is tired of her aimless flight, and sits on a Clematis flower. She sucks some dewdrops which are there since that morning, protected by the shadow of the house.

"If you spend your time in dreams, you'll get no more time to fulfil them..." These are the

words said by that fine white bush, which embraces the garden wall with a white cloud, a beautiful light cloud, which is well attached to it with the roots of a creeper....

"It's true", Chleo thinks," so much I like dreaming , that now the sun is low already, it's almost sunset...my life is going to finish without I did my job, the one which all the butterflies do: to help plants to pollinate, to lay eggs to give life to other butterflies....and now? Shall my life be over in this way, with this sense of emptiness, since I have never really lived it?"

The sun is at the sunset: now the flowers are closed, and the other butterflies are going to rest somewhere, to appreciate the last moments of light with the joy to did what it was right to do .... But perhaps she can still help someone, perhaps she can still do some job, before closing her wings forever. And Chleo sees, in the other side of the garden, a lit window, and, beyond the windowpane, a girl who chews a pencil, staring at the sunset.

Caroline, absorbed, is realizing that the day is almost over and that the geometric design has not been begun yet. How didn't she get aware of the hours passing? Surely, now she is not more eager than before, on the contrary the idea to begin that homework is, if possible, even more repulsive. If only she could be like that butterfly, flying without a thought, dipped in the sunset light, if only she could fly following her dreams, like she, playing with air and clouds....

On the contrary the butterfly , now, is not so carefree, but is dreadfully full of thoughts: she definitely wants to help someone , otherwise she will not die in peace. She begins beating her wings in front of the window, then she beat on the windowpane with the little legs, pretending not to see it , and trying to come in, knocking against it. Eventually, Caroline opens the window and Chleo rushes inside , going to sit just on the drawing paper, shaking her wings. Now , she does not know what to do. She only wants that black-haired could smile again. A drop has fallen from her wings in the middle of the sheet. Caroline tries to let the butterfly fly again, but Chleo, now, sturdy stays on her legs, like the Clematis was attached to the wall, and she cannot be displaced.

With her finger, Caroline picks up the drop which falled on the sheet; she bringit to the lips, wondering how come that butterfly stands there, still, instead of fluttering, light and dreaming.
The drop brings to Caroline the energy of the Clematis and of Chleo, and also Caroline's feet, now, are well attached to the ground; her eyes go to the watch and evaluate the time: half an hour to square the sheet and to draw the first lines, fifteen minutes to complete the project, and fifteen minutes for thefinal touches. Exactly one hour, and this is just the time lacking to the beginning of her favourite TV show. She goes, resolute, to switch the music off, and begins working. It might not be the garden of her dreams, anyway it will be a fine city park, with benches and swings, and lamps, and pic-nic tables, and trees, and flowers, and lawn to sit or lay down, looking to the clouds...and dreaming, yes, dreaming too....
The butterfly has moved aside, still on the windowsill, as if she were controlling Caroline's homework. When the work is finished, when Caroline bursts out in a hurrah! and in a wild dance, she understands that her

presence, someway, has been useful. She turns towards the last sunset sunrays, ready to accept the night. But, instead of feeling tired, as logic would, she feels that something strange is happening to her, her little legs are changing, her wings are becoming wider, and lighter, here comes two arms, and, on her side, a transparent bag, full of crumbled stars, or...YEEES, fairy dust! Chleo knows that sometimes this happens, they tell it in the woods and in the gardens, they tell that who help someone else who has a difficult time, without asking anything in exchange...then he is rewarded by Mother Nature....But she never expected all this: to become a fairy!

Thus, leaving behind herself a young girl dancing and her drawing completely finished in her schoolbag, Fairy Chleo turns to find a shelter for the night, near the Clematis who gave her a new life.

"The butterfly became fairy because she learned the lesson of Simplicity. The beauty is in each petal, in each leaf, in each pebble, in each city park...
Dreams are interesting exercises, but real life has so more vivid colours....."

Are you feeling anything on your face? Maybe the caresses of the clematis fairies, who greet you before flying away? Don't be sorry, you'll meet them again walking in the countryside, they'll be the Traveller's joy, so sweet and simple.

"Another vivid colour, the pink of the centaurea, shall be the colour of our next story..."

CENTAURY

What a hot July, this one! The field at hte border of the quarter is all dry. No shadow all around. Cecily frees Queen, her brother's dog. She decides to sit down, on the ground, waiting for her coming back: she is attracted magnetically by a beautiful plant with brilliant pink flowers, quiet in its beauty, even if around it there is so few green and so much heath.

Also today, as usual, it is Cecily's duty to carry out Queen. This habit began one day, after Mom went away in another town, to stay with her Aunt, who is ill. She left Cecily and her brother in the cares of the woman who cleans the house, Mrs Comandini. Her brother said that he was not aimed to carry out Queen, and Mrs Comandini too said that she did not want to, Queen looked at Cecily with imploring eyes, so that she offered herself. But since then, everybody supposed that she was the one who ought to carry out Queen, therefore Cecily hears rough words such as "Go out with Queen!" or "It's time for Queen to pee"... Cecily, sometimes likes to do so, and happily, and other times she doesn't like, but she does not succeed in telling it, and does it all the same. Like today. Like today, when she was immersed in a beautiful storybook sent by express mail by Mom. It s a book of famous stories: sure, some of them are already familiar to her, because she saw them as cartoon movies, but reading them is so different, such a lot of things come out from the story...besides that, now, it is no more time, for her, to watch TV. Since Mom's departure, her brother August ponkled himself in front of the TV, took possession of the remote control, and decides what to see and when to see. "Cartoons, pfui..." he says. Now they watch only fictions or videocassettes which Mrs Comandini considers "not proper for you"...Therefore, some evenings, after dinner, Mrs Comandini watches those movies with her brother, while Cecily washes the dishes, in the kitchen. A few minutes ago, she was just reading Cinderella. She has never succeeded in watching that cartoon movie, therefore she does not know the story. She seemed she was really there, with Cinderella, cleaning the fireplace ashes, and chatting with her little mice..it is quite the same when she chatters with her dolls, cleansing them and choosing their dresses and putting them on and off, and cares of them when they are ill, singing lullabies to let them fall asleep. What a pity that she did never spend such a beautiful night like the one of Cinderella with her prince...Well, there was that evening...when she went to Maggie's pijama party with all her friends, on her birthday...but she could not remain to sleep in Maggie's house, because Mrs Comandini did not allowed her to do so. Mrs Comandini told her she was not supposed to pass and catch her on the next morning, to accompany her to the school....Therefore, August came, the same night, laughing of all them watching a stupid horror film, with cakes and chips, and he took her away before the end of the film...

Well, she was reading that story, and she was at the point when Cinderella is locked in a room so that she can't fit the shoe, when the two voices of August and Mrs Comandini, in a perfect chorus, imposed her to carry out Queen...Now she would like to hurry up, to run home and finish the story, because she is afraid that the end will not be happy at all. Sometimes these old times stories end melanconically, and she would like to tear the book's pages and to rewrite the ending, but...she is sorry for the book, for her Mom, who gave it to her, who could be saddened... Her eyes go on staring at the plant's pink flowers: it is the same color she fancies Ciderella's beautiful dress. Pink is the color of goodness, and Cinderella surely is a good girl, because she always does what she is asked for, never complaining. Like Cecily is supposed to do, when Mrs Comandini asks her to clean the bathroom, and to hang the washing, and to wash dishes, or to sweeps the rooms, to carry out the garbage, to make her bed and August's.....while sometimes she would almost tell her that Mom gave Mrs Comandini the duty to do all this, not Cecily...and that sometimes she wishes to play, also, or to read...she would almost tell her....almost.... Cecily takes out of her rugsack Queen's bowl, and the flusk with fresh water. What a desire to sip some water: it is so fresh! But surely Queen is more thirsty than she is, and moreover her brother insisted so much to make Queen drink a lot. She puts the bowl under the little plant that she likes so much, so that her shadow can keep cool the water. The, she pours the water in the bowl, letting it flow over the plant, and refreshing her flowers too: she too is hot, surely, and so, with the same water, she offers a service to both: plant and dog.

Now Queen arrives, panting, and jumpes in front of her bowl. She sips almost all, leaving only some on the bottom, and then she run away again.....Then, Cecily negotiates whith her thirst and dips her fingers in the water, passing them, after that, on her face, to refresh herself, and sucking some drops. And Centaury, the pink-flowered plant, who poured her essence in the bowl, gets deeply into Cecily, and makes her feel different, as she wore a magic pink dress. She makes her feel just like her: so shining and beautiful, to whom is able to see, even it is not apparent, at a first look. So unique, neither servant, nor queen, simply herself, proud to be so and to be able to do of her life all what she wants. She likes to be a help for other, this is sure, but she does not want to find herself drinking the leftovers of her brother's dog! Cecily takes the remaining water and pours it on her head, to finally refresh herself. The, with a firm voice, calls "Queen, come here! Let's go home!" and, resolute and fast, she leashes Queen, pulling her when she stops to smell something. She wants to hurry up to come back, she is eager to finish the story. While she is walking home, she thinks, more deeply than she can. " Go on, Cinderella, free yourself from your prison, let your voice be heard, tell that it was you, that night, tell that you do not want any more do homework for your sisters-in –law, retake your life and your freedom..." And Cecily is still thinking this, repeating it over and over again, when she get in her bedroom, after leaving Queen to her brother with the words " Last time I carry her out with this hot!". She jumps on the book, opens it at the last pages of the story, and , hurrah, she finds out that Cinderella too realized that she has the same rights as every other; that she suceeds in telling that the shoe is hers, and that, eventually, she does not become bad, but , on the contrary, she remains a very good girl! In fact she arranges marriages for the sisters- in-law, and forgives her mother-in –law...

Cecily closes the book, happily. She goes into the living-room, where Mrs Comandini is watching TV, and says to her: "Today I decided not to clean the kitchen. I prefer to write a letter to Mom, so that I can tell her something of me, of us...."

"Sure, sure..." Mrs Comandini mumbles, standing up " I know that it falls all to me .." But, what a strange thing, she eventually goes into the kitchen, and her brother invites Cecily to sit besides him, on the sofa. It has been sufficient to say it! And, smiling, Cecily thinks "...therefore Cecily lived happy forever, with all her loved ones...."

"Did you think that to get the virtue of Force, you ought to be big or tall? The lesson of the centaury is clear: if you are small and humble, no enemies can notice you, and your force shall be huge...
We fairies are masters in littleness...and will be able to nurtur the little flowers of centaurea with the Force of the Universe..
And when the pink becomes violet, the inapparence becomes evidence: this is the case of the gentian...."

GENTIAN

Jack and his uncle had been walking in the mountains for a while. It was the end of the vacation, and Jack had agreed to go on this walk only after his uncle's insistence. As far as he was concerned he really didn't feel like making the effort, sure that later on his muscles would be sore and his feet covered in blisters…in any case the situation down at the holiday camp had been lost: Jade, the girl that he fancied wasn't paying any attention to him whatsoever, and actually it was very likely that right now she was making fun of him with her girlfriends. And he certainly didn't want to make another effort, after making a fool of himself yesterday. His uncle must know, as he couldn't avoid occasional sighs, especially when the subject turned to girls….finally he told him the whole story, and the reply was the usual thing that grown-ups said, those with a beard and a bit of muscle. How he wished he could turn back , maybe go to his room, curl up and read comic books, far from everybody and everything! Just as he taking off his backpack abruptly, ready to make this very suggestion to his uncle…"Watch out!" his uncle yells, grabbing hold of his arm – "you are about to set it down on that Gentian"'" He points to a plant sticking out straight in the low grass, with clusters of purple flowers and elongated leaves. How could he have ignored it, it's so solid and colourful! Jack puts his knapsack down somewhere else, feeling awkward and clumsy as usual, and sits down next to it, too tired to tell his uncle what he is thinking: that in any case, whatever he does, Jade will surely not speak to him any more, so what was the point in trying, especially two days before the end of the vacation……….

What neither the uncle nor Jack could however see is that a little fairy dressed in purple, scared and excited, had taken flight from under the gentian leaves hiding her, and was flying agitatedly around them, thinking: "They almost squashed my plant! It's really true that when we are unhappy we only see ourselves and not the marvels surrounding us….poor boy! Thank goodness this handsome cowboy thought of saving my life!", the fairy says sitting down on the uncle's wide-brimmed hat, with a wicked twinkle in her eye. "He will have his reward: three wishes granted, I promise!"

The uncle continues his sermon on women: "so you see, women play hard to get, they want to be courted…don't give up, keep trying and you'll win". The fairy on the hat smoothes her hand through her hair and says "Men!, shrugging her shoulders and crossing her legs to be more comfortable, waiting to fulfil her promise. The path continues to rise, seemingly endless, making Jack doubt whether there really is a refuge.

"That's it, I'm tired, I don't feel like going on", Jack says, coming to a halt, discouraged. "I'll never be able to go up all that way", gazing at the rest of the winding path on the map.

"Come now", his uncle encourages him, "a delicious lunch will be awaiting our arrival at the refuge".

"But you didn't even call to book" Jack interrupts, "how can you be sure that there will be something to eat?"

"Something to eat?!", his uncle replies shocked, "more than that, I'm telling you there will be a feast! Have faith!"

Jack resumes walking , and replies in a somewhat sceptical tone: "All right, but what does *have faith* mean? "Holy cow! Now that's some question!" the uncle thinks, lifting his hat to scratch his head. "And now how can I explain faith to him, something that you either have or don't have? How I wish I had the right words...."

The Gentian fairy who is whirling around him, listening to his thoughts, breaks out in a delighted smile: "There, your first wish!" And immediately enters the uncle's thought cloud, sweeping away all the useless words and spraying fairy powder. The uncle hears words that he didn't think of issuing from his mouth, and while he himself listens to them for the first time, he says to Jack:

"You shouldn't think that faith is something that belongs to you. It is rather a choice. If you were sure of something, because you had tried it- for example if you had seen the refuge's menu and had made a booking *– you wouldn't need to have faith. You would have a certainty. Rather it is doubt that urges you towards faith. Every morning, when you wake up, and begin to have doubts, you have two possibilities:*

chose to have faith that everything will work out for the best, or chose to think that things will go wrong. And you know what man's greatest freedom is? That only he decides what to chose. I recommend number one: the day is much easier and happier…it's much better, trust me!" "Or not?" the uncle thinks, somewhat perplexed. "Did what I say make any sense? And what did I say?" Looking at Jack's slightly confused face he realizes that something in his look has changed, but that could simply be an expression of "poor uncle, he's getting old, these hikes reduce the oxygen supply to his brain, he's not as lucid as he used to be…."; nevertheless his walk is brisker now. He continues to think: "how I wish he could understand what I just said to him, how I wish he could find trust and faith in his gut, without trying to understand it through words, which I am not even sure were mine…" The Gentian fairy pricks up her ears. "Good! A second wish! In the gut, he said?" She quickly pulls out a few ready-to-use petals of Gentian from the pouch around her neck, and taking advantage of a stop to pee, she lets them drop into Jack's water flask, left open on a rock in the sun next to the knapsack.

Jack comes back, and is drinking in little sips, so that his water ration may last as long as possible (something tells him it won't last to the last uphill stretch), and for the third time says to his uncle: "I can just see the two of us arriving at the refuge, with our tongues hanging out, only to find out that they don't do restaurant service…you know what I think uncle?" But he interrupts his sentence midway, because all of a sudden the answer to his question has just taken shape in his gut….actually it's as if his gut is speaking: "I think they will have mushroom noodles and wild berry pie, which I will order together with a hot chocolate and whipped cream…I can already feel it melting in my mouth…let's go uncle, what are you waiting for? Aren't you hungry?"

His uncle sees him red in the face as he puts on his knapsack, and takes off for the last climb, and can't believe his ears or eyes: Jack has discovered faith! Ok it's faith in noodles, berries and chocolate, but it's still faith….

"Well", the uncle thinks as he tries to keep up with Jack, "and if there was nothing of the kind at the refuge? And what if the restaurant were really closed? How I wish Jack's favourite menu was really there awaiting us!

"A piece of cake!" the fairy thinks "here is your third wish!" And with a beating of wings she takes off for the refuge, to set the table......

"Which is the role of doubt in our lives? Sometimes it is an obstacle against optimism, sometimes it is the ground where the plant of Prudence flourishes. Is there any of you who likes proceeding in small steps? Is there any scientist fairy who observes and collects data, and, with, prudence, finally uses them to show God's design?
Good-bye, little gentian fairies...the mountain meadows are waiting for you...."

Stay with me, don't fly away, you're not a fairy..
Not yet, anyway. Open you eyes, cautiously, and you could see violet sparks flying in the night, to their new lives...
Now, again, open your heart, to fairy Violet's next story....

VERVAIN

"This year we must win!" Victor thinks while going to the meeting of the August holiday celebration Committee, in the Communal Council. Here, the delegations of all the municipality divisions gathered, and Victor participates as schoolboys representative. Now, at this meeting, he continuously raises his hand, and proposes the same thing: a seven-a side football tournament as the main attraction of the celebrations. He already imagines his party (the higher district of the village), the red-blue, overcome the green-blu (the district near the railway station, in the lower part of the village). It shall need a real intensive training, he's sure, but he already knows whom he'll call in the team. And, while the adults of the Committee don't dare what to object anything against this young keen boy (who already said that he himself will prepare the pitch, and will train the team, and that they will not be bored by any other detail), Veronica, the representative of the schoolgirls, intervenes as soon as she is allowed to, to say that in this way, girls will not be able to play, and , instead a treasure hunt could be a more appropriate play....Yes, she speaks aloud too, but Victor does it more, thus the Committee meeting concludes with an OK to the football proposal. Swoing indifference to the complaints of Veronica, who tries to stop him at the exit, Victor rushes to his district, where he rins the bells of a dozen candidate football players, wrenching them to a lazy afternoon and to TV cartoons watched in the fresh living-room gloom. "Because", he urges them " it's time to begin the training, up!" Without being influenced by their resistance, he convinces them to come out and to begin warming up with a light race down and up from the church to the station and return, stating that the breath is the most important thing, for the victory....

But, at the top of the climb, getting to the church, Victor turns down and sees that he lost half of the team at the icecream shop, and that the rest of it, red and in a sweat, have scarsely the breath to say: "Tomorrow, rest..."

"We'll talk again about it!" He shouts, departing, because his projects need another step: a fine pitch, where they could train themselves, and, finally palin the longed tournament. While going in the suburbs of the village, Victor thinks whom he could ask to, for the team uniforms: his aunt, and his friend's grandmother can sew; they'll be easily convinced....No problem, he sings under the hot afternoon sun....

Victor finds a large uncultivated land, which could become a wonderful pitch.

"Up, at work!" He thinks, and begins pulling out the weeds, to free the area. At the edge of the field there is a group of fine Vervain plants, under which a flower fairy is sleeping, hidden among the leaves. The vervain plant started with fear, and this suddenly awakens her fairy, who notices a coming danger: a boy, got wet and heated is getting nearer and nearer, unperturbed, uprooting any plant he meets. He mumbles something that sounds like a football-game commentary: " Then, the centre-forward starts and kicks a powerful shot, overtakes the green-blue goalkeeper...Goal! it is goal, and game for the red-blues!!!" With this shout, he fiercly uproots a bush of weed. The danger gets nearer: the fairy quickly flies to Victor, and, not seen, (her flight is so fast that only very careful eyes could notice it) she unlaces

Victor's shoes, who stumbles and stops. But only for a while, in order to lace them again. Then , like a panzer, he goes on towards her plant. So, now, a tug at his shirt, now a bells' sound, which cause him to turn to understand what is happening, now a pinch to his leg, which makes him to fight the insect which pricked him, and to lick the biting . A small obstacle after another, Fairy Vervain tries to stop him, but her attempts are not very effective. Nothing could arrest the vision of grandeur in which Victor is immersed, when his team, eventually, will win the August tournament, and the red-blue flags will wave in the main road until the first autumn rains. Fairy vervain wipes her sweat with her perfumed lilac little handkerchief. "This young boy is really fanatic " she thinks "he never stops...under this hot sun he moves as if something inside pushed him, something which never lets up, which makes him not to feel pain or strain...he ought to learn a lesson from my plant, who is so passionate in her growing that she forgets behind her leaves, rising up with her subtle stalks, but then she stops, in a quiet and lilac peace, with her small spikes turned to the sky, delicate and inapparent, even if they keep their self- confidence...."

Fairy Vervain profits by a moment in which Victor has stopped, looking behind all the work done, and she keeps flying over his head, squeezing her handkerchief and putting it again around her forehead, to get her hair away. Some drops of her sweat sprinkle on Victor, who, surprised, watches at the blue sky, looking for any passing cloud. The, he wipes his forehead and face and passes his hand over his mouth. They are salty drops, and it's like they were, say, lilac-coloured, so peaceful is the emotion they make him feel. Suddenly, Victor wants to stop, just here, near these plant that is to be pulled off....and the wish to uproot it, how strange, is no more here, as if it were overcome by a sense of friendliness and protection towards this small flower raising up, with no leaves, with its delicate spike.

Maybe, thinking better, the pitch is large enough, and, even if it does not look like an official football field, it is wide, and invites toplay...yes, to play also different games....Victor feels strange, light, free to think lots of possibilities....to game ....

"Prisoner handball! Why couldn't we play a prisoner handball tournament?" he hears the voice of Veronica's little sister, talking with her. And Veronica, answering: "Any game, but football, it is a game for boys, only they can play it..." Veronica stops to pick up a Vervain flower, and, while thinking, distractly chews the spike, as if it were her pencil, as she does usually.

"Or..." she continues, inspired..

" A terrific race in the sacks!" Victor bursts out, amazing himself and Veronica.

"And an obstacle race, in teams, "Veronica adds " as a relay race..and one of the proofs could be in kicking a penalty...or do you think that will be too difficult for girls?"

"Well, I think that you could succeed in kicking a penalty..come with me, let me teach to you..."

Victor and Veronica go away with Victor's ball and Veronica's sister, behind them, rubs her eyes: she cannot believe what she sees...a litlle winged being, with the dress sleeves well rolled up, and a lilac band around the forehead, is flying after them, passing from one to another, happily clapping hands and wings.....

"So small the spikes of that flower, so great the virtue of Patience. How great is the need of Tolerance in human hearts....I hope that many of you will embrace that virtue...so that each litlle vervain flower will be cared and nurtured by the fairies' love.
Our peolple can teach tolerance to the human race: The value of difference has been taught to us since our first steps in the game of lives. We well know that each different existence has its own reason...
But how can we teach to trust in this truth?
This is the matter of the next story....."

CERATO

"No, no, you cannot move Cerato!." Beyond the fence, Anna's voice, his neighbour, is claiming to the gardener, who advised her to move the plant in the other side of the garden.
Charlie, sitting on the steps of his door, instinctively compares the resolute tone of his neighbour, seemingly so old and fragile, with the continuous exitations of Mom, whom the gardener would have convinced since a lot of time in moving cerato, ivy, cubbage, and the whole house too.....
" I absolutely do not want to move it: it is my daily gift!"
Charlie, become curious, as soon as the gardener goes away, passes the fence and asks to Anna what does "the daily gift" mean.
"It is the gift that every day I receive: often there are more than one gift, all different. You know, if I let Cerato in this position, every morning, in this period, when I open my eyes, I can see it from my bed, when I awake....And so, the day gives a gift to me, at once....Look how beautiful it is, with those blue and violet

flowers...Do you know this plant comes from Tibet?"

"Tibet....is the world's roof...I studied it!"

"So it is...It is so high that from there you can hear very well God's voice...or the voice of Anyone who is over the clouds...."

Charlie listens to her, puzzled; therefore Anna explains:"That particular voice which you can not hear with your ears, but with your heart....Tell me, you didn't receive any gift, today, did you?, since you look so confused and depressed...."

Charlie explains that since fifteen days he has to chose the optional subjects, before the beginning of the new school : "I passed all these days in talking with the teachers, and with the older students, and with Mom who asks for advice to her friend, and with the caretakers, and..."

"And with that Smorf which was here the day before yesterday, don't you? Come on, don't make that face, I know that you think that we adults do not see smorfs, but it is not true...Sometimes we pretend not to see them, not to scare children.....but what did he tell you, finally?"

"Nothing, nothing....because when you talk to them, to smorfs, they usually go away...and so, now, there lasts only one more day to the beginning of the school, and I did not yet decide anything...."

"There is time, yet...I know, my nephew Rocco told me, that school begins in a couple of weeks..."

"Not my school..." Charlie says " I go to a special school, which begins before the others, and has some more subjects. Mom suggested it to me, because Edward's father suggested to her, and in effect Edward seems happy to frequent it.....but today I have to choose the subjects and I don't know how..."

"Well, this means that today it's me that will give you a daily gift..." And Mrs Anna cuts some cerato flower and gives them to Charlie, as if , with that simple act, she could solve all his uncertainties.

But, you know, old people are always a little odd. Charlie puts the flowers in a vase on his bedside table, and then he passes the rest of the afternoon and the evening searching in Internet all kind of information which could help him in deciding of his student's life.

His mother, in the other room, is talking by phone to a friend of her, saying a long series of "yes, yes, sure, it could be a good idea...and what about changing the colour of the sofa?" and so on.

A question mark after another, in a rhythm which makes Charlie sleepy, and eager to lie down on his bed.

A restless sleep catches him as soon as he closes his eyes: the voices of each person that gave advice to him get mixed in his head and take the shape of a lot of characters, around him, in a classroom.

Someone is running around the desks, someone is climbing the walls...He sees Mom with her phone sticked on her ear, Edward with a magnifying lens, Edward's father building a cards castle with his foot while reading the newspaper, Rocco and Piercarlo ply with a ball in a corner..

.He sees the teachers of the new school; the music teacher who throws the violin's strings as if they were rubbers, and the biology teacher who is training a team of ants...and everyone is talking, talking, talking....

Charlie is tossing, sweated, and stretches out his hand towards the bedside table, knocking the vase. Some petals of cerato fall down, in the glass of water the Mom everyday puts for him on the table, in the case he were thirsty.

And, in fact, after a while, his thirst becomes really burning, and Charlie drinks the whole glass, to find some peace in his mouth, and in his dream, too. And he turns himself on the other side, going on dreaming...

So it happens, in the dream, that the door opens and the school caretaker, whose face is like ...yes, is like Anna's face!..., says, with a serious tone:

" Seat everyone! The new Teacher has come!" and she lets place to a tall figure, with oriental features, dressed in blue and violet, just like the flowers that Fabrizio was given . His face is smiling, nevertheless nobody dares to breathe. And, standing in front of the class, he says aloud:

"Lao Tzu says:

Only three things I have to teach: simplicity, patience, compassion.

*These are your greatest treasures.
If you are simple in your actions
and thoughts,
you return to the life essence.
If you are patient with friends and
enemies,
you move in harmony with what is
happening.
If you are full of love and
compassion towards yourself,
you bring peace
to all living beings."*

In the classroom the silence welcomes the Teacher's speech, and changes Charlies's dream in a deep and quiet sleep, until the morning.

What a night! Charlies gets up, strectching out, and the flowers the he sees on his table make him smile: here it is his daily gift! But he received another one , too. His mind, now , is clearer: all the dreams of the night carried away his uncertainties, and what he can hear now, strong and clear, while going into the kitchen, is a voice coming right from his heart.

"Mom, finally I decided!" and goes on, smiling, " I decided,, eventually, that I do not want to go to the special school: there are less holidays, and much more subjects...On the contrary, I want to go to school with Rocco and his friends: they are always so happy, when I meet them, at the football field..

"Are you really sure?" Mom says, very puzzled " yesterday Edward's father told me about the working opportunities opened by the knowledge of one more language..."

"Mom, I know two thing with extreme certainty: I do not want to frequent that school, and, second, that you better go to take a tea with Mrs Anna, one of these days, even today, if you can...".

Charlie, now, feels himself so light, light such as if he were in high mountain, or, better, on a very high mountain, on the roof of the world....

"Really, the virtue of Faith makes richer each breathe, each step, each moment, and the Wisdom can convince reason to kneel in front of Faith.
Deep in the human heart, a wise voice can always speak....Which of you would like to amplify these voices? Easy duty in children, more difficult in grown up...in any case, a way which leads to independence...A rare gift, like rare are the plants of cerato....Take care of them, please...."

Don't you hear the music, now? Might it be our inner voices, resounding like a harp? Or, rather, the sound of Tibetan bells inviting us to meditation?
Make silence, so that Fairy Violet can tell another story....

IMPATIENS

In the house of Family Quick, Mrs. Constance is trying to explain to her son Daniel the solution of the math exercise. "Understood, understood!" he exclames, and run away to his room. Daniel is called *Speedy* by his baseball team, as he is a runner and he is unbeatable when he runs from a base to another, to achieve a home-run. Constance shakes her head. How can he have understood, she not even explained the beginning of the execution....

Daniel is writing the solution oh his exercise book. Mom is too slow in explaining things. He always knows the end of each of her sentences, but she does not understand it, and wants to finish the same. The, when she realize that he *really* understood, ends by getting angry, saying "If you do not listen to the others, nobody will listen to you!...." Now, for instance, she is calling him into the kitchen, and, with the knife in her hand, while she is chopping the lettuce, she tells him that, since yesterday she has not found Ike, and that maybe....Daniel already knows that she wants him to go and find him, and darts out into the garden without saying a word, leaving her shouting "Where are you going ,now?...."

Ike, the home turtle, decided to leave. Since too much time he has been in this garden. From beyond the fence, an ineffable call comes to him. The wish to explore, to go forward, to run towards adventure, put on him an almost uneasy restlessness. The wish to run, become greater and greater in his legs, makes him to push his head forward, more and more, towards the future, which is waiting for him; but the inadequacy of his muscles holds him back. So, ahead, struggling, with strain, angry with his body which is not up to his wish to run, anyway ahead, ahead, never resting....During a short stop to breathe Ike notices, nearby, a pink-violet spot, a group of odd flowers... "Yesterday, here, there was nothing of this, and today, suddenly, leaves, flowers and seeds quite ripened! Gosh, what a speed! What a fine example to emulate! Who knows if, eating some of these flowers, their energy could recharge me, give me their same uncontainable vitality..." And, thinking this, Ike's mouth reaches the most tender and pink of those flowers, picks up some petals, chews and swallows them, like a sacred rite.

"To every thing there is a season, and a time to every purpose under the heaven:
a time to sprout, a time to flower;
a time to run, a time to stop."

In Ike's head these words resound, heavy like stones. And from his head they fall down, widen under his shell, and descend in the legs, making them heavier, even stitching them to the ground....What? *Time to stop*, the words are telling... But he had fed himself of that flower so energic, so dynamic, to go faster!...But now, that heavy feeling in the legs melts, and his fatigued and hardened muscles relax, becoming tender and giving to him a peaceful sensation. Delightfully, everything around him becomes more coloured, sharper. Details appair never noticed before: that small snail hanging from a grass thread, that fine white butterfly, over there, having a waltz, following her own music, the earth's scent, and that queue of ants crossing his way...how come, before, did he not become aware of these wonders? Sure that, so looking, the garden is really a world rich of surprise, and the wide lands beyond the fench could wait some more time...and Ike begins strolling, for the first time in his life. In the meanwhile, Speedy is on trail's Ike. Following the deductive method described in the book he recently devoured (Sherlock Holmes and Baskerville curse), he already found the first traces, a lettuce leaf half chewed dropped some feet near the bowl. To leave there his favourite food, Ike should have hurried up...(*oh, yes, Watson!*), therefore we ought to follow the line between bowl and lettuce...here a small crushed branch...here, near this group of brilliant pink flowers, Speedy Sherlock notices some flattened grass . Looking better, he sees that some of them have been nibbled. And, deducing it from the sizes of the bites, it ought to be an animal greater than a snail and smaller than the Baskerville mastiff...maybe a male turtle weighing aproximately three ounces (*elementary, Watson!*). Now we shall investigate more: we must put ourselves in one's shoes, and to do this...yes, a detective must be ready for anything, must do exactly what the subject did....Daniel hesitates a while, then he picks up some petals of those fine pink-violet flowers and chew them, laid on the ground, just as Ike probably had done. In effect, something happens...because there, from that low point of view, he not only discovers perfumes, colours and unexpected amazing details, but also he sees, just in front of him, lined up with his nose, Ike's small tail slowly moving, with his steps' rhythm.. a rhythm which is different from his usual plodding, almost a rapper rhythm....Is it really him? "Ike!" Daniel cries at him, laughing. And Ike, with that same rhythm, neither fast nor slow, turns and....winks at him.

"Mummy! I found Ike...I think it's him.. It seems him...but he's....SUPER!" Daniel laughs, and he cannot explain to Mom anything of what happened, also because, in effect, nothing special happened....

Mrs Constance, who is still chopping the lettuce, looks askance at him and begins to say, as if she did not interrupt her previous conversation: "Well, well.. After all what I did to find a ground turtle for you, and what I do to give him fresh lettuce..." Constance goes on, lowering her voice and mumbling, because she already knows that Daniel will not listen to her anymore, since he'll have run to his room....on the contrary, with the corner of her eye, she notices him there, quite still, LISTENING..and then telling her, with a smile: "True, Mom, thank you. I know you really do a great job".

Mrs. Constance stops, without saying a word: she does not believe to what is happening: As usual, Daniel could have told each single word of what she was going to say, but he finally realized that she only wanted to be listened to. Because she did not really care the Daniel understood her words, she most wished TO SAY them, to pour them in someone's ears.

And, for this time, Daniel offered his ears. Now that Mom's words are finished (so soon?), Daniel can go to his room, neither fast nor slow, but walking with the right time beaten inside him:

I-KE, I-KE….

"Are you eager to dare the wide world, do you want to dare the unknown, do you want to dare God, like Ike? If this is the case, then you need the virtue of Fear of God....That fear can be a great help to you, in many a case, such as challenge can be an obstacle, too, in other cases...Human sages told there was a time to live and a time to die...know your time, live it completely, trusting in what that time will bring to you, in each twinkling of eyes, in each beat of wings....Good bye, little devas, blessed be your journeys through the time and beyond the time....But other kinds of fear are real obstacles in many a case, too...And there comes the virtue of Hope...Listen to the story of Helianthemum....

ROCK ROSE

Mr. Rochette yawned while he searched for his car keys. He yawned again while he parked the car near the office. Then he walked with a restless step towards his desk while he continued to ask himself: "How is it possible that Rocco who is already grown continues to wake up every night with nightmares? And even during the day he is no longer himself, he seems terrified by something....but by what?"

Rocco, his son, walked listlessly towards school. He wouldn't get there on time today either. It was as if his legs didn't want to move and slowed down just to spite him. Once again he heard the bell ringing, and there he was still standing before the entrance. "Let's hope the teacher isn't too angry" he thought to himself, resigned to being late.

In the early afternoon sun Grandma was taking little Rose to the park. Rose was reflecting on the previous night. Like on so many nights before this one, just as she was deep in what seemed like everlasting sleep, she (and not only she) was awoken by the terrified screams of her brother Rocco. She tried to help him:

immediately she got out of bed and went to his aid, bringing him Rabbit (his stuffed yellow rabbit) and putting it in his bed. But though Rocco looked at it with tenderness, his movements betrayed irritability, as if to say (yes, it was as if she could read Rocco's thoughts) that a rabbit, by definition a coward who flees at the mere sound of noise, could never give him the courage to face and defeat monsters. Well, thought Rose, first of all it is a yellow rabbit, not just any rabbit, and besides it surely can't take much to make that Smorf in the corner of Rocco's room flee. It isn't even one of the worst kind...
Suddenly Rose's face lit up. Grandma knew that face. No fighting it. So when Rose insisted on having Grandma buy her a lollipop, she purchased it without arguing.
The sun was just setting and the gates of the park have been closed. The urban fairies are whispering excitedly among themselves, and one of them pulls out a yellow lollipop, found in the trunk of their tree. The lollipop then presents Rose 's request to the fairies, and right away they know that this is a job for Eli, a mountain fairy, from the mountain that can be

seen off to the North, light blue against an almost dark blue sky. The crow that is trotting around in the area takes flight while the fairies prepare to welcome a guest, making space in their tree and spreading fresh daisy petals on the clean bed.

And then Eli arrives, smiling and dishevelled, but beautiful in her yellow outfit. She gets off the crow wings, shortly afterwards taking flight again (with her wings this time as the trip is a shorter one) in direction of the semi-open window of the Rochette family home, or more specifically Rocco's room.

Eli looks at Rocco with his eyes closed, his mouth slightly open, his body occasionally racked with trembles. Every once in a while the shaking of his arms and legs reveal the intensity of his dreams. His fists are closed and his legs rigid: poor little one, what kind of terrible adventure is he on? Then Eli thinks of the Rock Rose, the flower of her home, up there in the mountains. She thinks of its *courage*, so small and fragile, yet nevertheless capable of withstanding snow and rain storms. She thinks of the ability of its small roots to penetrate into the rock, growing where other flowers are unable to survive. She thinks of the colour yellow and of its petals, of the sparks of yellow that illuminate the grey of the rock, so small and yet so vibrant, and which open the heart with a smile. She feels such a longing for her home, her small flower, that suddenly tears fill her eyes. Then, plop, plop..two tear droplets fall on the semi-open mouth of Rocco, right on his tongue. Rocco closes his mouth in his sleep, sucks in Eli's tears... and something changes. Eli watches Rocco's face relax, the mouth almost curving into a smile. His eyes open, he is awake. Quickly she hides behind the curtains.

Rocco rises quickly almost laughing, and goes straight over to the corner of the room where a shapeless form has grown, night after night, taking on a monstrous shape in his dreams. And he asks: "Who are you? Want do you want from me? Look at my courage now, and answer me, or I will destroy you with the snap of my fingers..." The shadow replies. No words can be heard, but the answer is clearly formed in Rocco's mind (and Eli's, who continues to observe the scene): "I don't know who I am..I only know that your fear nurtured me and made me grow..and that is what I want..I only want your attention…I will go away..but don't hurt me…" The shadow slithers out of the room, getting smaller and smaller.

Rocco looks around, satisfied. He likes his room. The posters on the wall, the shoes thrown under the desk, underpants and socks heaped in a stack on the floor.. and the corners of the room finally vacant and clean. There is a strange glow behind the curtains….who knows, maybe it's the light of the stars. Yawning and stretching, he gets back under the sheets and falls asleep.

All is quiet in the Rochette residence. It is shortly before sunrise, and the noise of the first buses in the street can be heard. But in the silence, THE SCREAM: no not the usual scream, but ONE scream. Which comes from the room of Mr. Rochette. Mr. Rochette realizes that the scream came from his mouth and sits up, terrified. What happened? What is making his teeth chatter for fear, what is tying his stomach up in a knot? He hears the bare feet of Rose pitter-pattering down the hallway, now the yellow rabbit is being shoved in his

bed, and he feels the blankets being tucked in as well. Then almost as if Rose has had second thoughts, he feels her getting in the bed too, and whispering to him "don't be scared daddy, I will take care of it tomorrow..".
Just for a moment before falling back to sleep, Mr. Rochette is aware that Rocco did not wake up tonight.

Mr. Rochette yawns while he looks for the car keys. And continues to yawn while he parks the car near the office. He walks restlessly towards his desk, as if the nighttime fear still had a hold on him.
Rocco slips into the classroom just as the bell rings. "Rochette, again…", but the teacher does not finish her sentence. Before her is a beaming Rocco. Not missing a beat he takes of his satchel and sits down at his desk before the bell has finished ringing.
Eli is sleeping in the tree trunk, a guest of the urban fairies. Here the air is denser than in the mountain, and not at all fragrant, but she is so happy to have helped Rocco…a smile creeps over her mouth while she sleeps, and at every breath her happiness causes fairy powder to

spread over her folded wings, making them glow.

In the early afternoon sun, Grandma takes Rose to the park: Rose tugs her coat: "Grandma, I want a lollipop.." Grandma, resigned, lets herself be pulled toward the bar, while she grumbles: "today as well? And perhaps yellow too?"

"Little yellow brave fairies, good bye.....I wish you to water your flowers with the virtue of Hope, which gives the courage to face each difficulty....

And you, who are still here, aren't you afraid to remain alone? If you are here, this meams that loneliness is your way, just like the water violet, who grows alone....."

WATER VIOLET

Fairy Violet still reminds when she was leaning on Raven's back, hugging a water violet plant, to protect themselves from the wind. They had been living together until the day before, in a remote, quiet water-course, in peaceful loneliness, far from the noises of the town, of the people, of the chattering of other plants and fairies (surely they are pleasant, but in small quantities). Then, unfortunately, the diggers did come to till and prepare the ground to build upon it; thus, she had to escape in a hurry. The city fairies had sent to them Raven, their high velocity means of transport, to carry her to their city park. She had just the time to take with her the water violet, wrapping her in a wet cloth, to protect her until their arrive.

Now they live here, in this city park, in the hollow of a yew trunk, where she cut out a space all for herself. She could not share her house with the other fairies, so chattering and noisy, not used to their silence, where even a flea, sliding on the water, makes a noise. Now she looks at the violet, immersed in a glass of water, who has begun again to stay right, lightening up the room with the pale lilac light of her flowers. She herself, can make more light than a daisy field! Fairy Violet is so proud to be her fairy, that she cannot imagine anyone like her in the world. But the flower corolla swings slowly, as if it were a shaking head, and the flower begins to talk: *"I know you feel yourself different from the other fairies; I know you feel them noisy; I know youare tryingy to stay here with me, secluded in this trunk, as if we were in our sheet of water. But if i's the peace what you are looking for, if it's the harmony of the water and of the green what you are longing and you are trying to recreate, this is not the way. It's not by closing the entrance to this room that you'll find the peace, but, on the contrary, it's by bringing our sheet of water out of here. Open the door of this room, open the door of your hearth, and let the music of our silence go out, let the delicate colours of my petals, the harmony of lines mirroring in the water go out. Let them go out, and let them mix, like a grain of sand, with the other grains that are out of here, Do it with humility, knowing that to be a shore, the shore needs of all the grains, and that yours, ours, is indispensable, as the others, in our smallness."* Fairy Violet, hearing these words, turns back and peeps out of a small hole of the trunk, looking, in evening becoming night, the first lights of the fairies , ready to the usual night chats, and tales and laughters. She finds some of them really rough, their laughters are unrefined, other ones ought to be on diet, to lighten their flight. Of course, it's true that none of them did ever know *her* world, and cannot appreciate silence, elegance, beauty, but...no, she reallay does not succeed in *opening the door* (as her flower is still whispering in her ears). And Fairy Violet brings her hands to the ears, not to listen anymore. But, just before covering them, she has the time to hear three more words, which she would have never listened: *"Tonight I 'll die..."*. So, opening her eyes wide, suddenly full of tears, she turns towards the flower, who continues: *"This is no more my place, but I still can be useful, even if my sacrifice is needed. I'll live through you, if you'll be able to open the door of your hearth , to tell the world about me."* Slowly, a petal after the other, two, three, petals fall in the water. Fairy Violet hurles herself to hug her plant, and soon finds her hands dipped in the water, picking up her petals and bringing to her mouth, kissing them. The water wets her face, together with her tears, and, like a combination lock, click after click, the door of the fairy's hearth opens, and the flower's spirit gets in her: the joy of the freedom that appears when loneliness is no more solitude but company of herself, the wish to give her own light to others, humbly. In the same way, with the same easiness, the door of the trunk's hollow opens and Fairy Violet goes out, elegantly flying, welcomed by happy cheers. "Finally you are here! We were just wondering when you could teach to us your special way of flying, so elegant, like that of a Fairy Queen....We were just planning an all night long lesson, if you are willing to teach....moreover, now that you're living here, you could join our team for children's help...your talent is precious... you know, you radiates a special peace, it is af if a sheet of water followed you, and our emotions could mirror in it and calm down," Fairy Violet's tears add to the sheet of water that surrounds her, and increase her light , "and besides, they not only calm down, but also are hold, hugged with love and humblity..."

Late afternoon, when Fairy Violet wakes up: it is unbelievable that she suceeded in sleeping, with such a children's noise outside! It has been the first quiet sleep since she arrived here. Near her bed, rolled up on the ground, one of the smallest fairies: think, a daisy!, which last night remained near her, in adoration, refusing to go back to the lawn. Well, she hopes this will not become a habit, but, for this night, the little fairy did not give her too many troubles. Fairy Violet looks at the glass of water in which the violet dissolved except for some petals. She still feels her vibrant spirit inside, she knows that her plant would not like stately burial ceremonies, but only to can remain at disposal, humbly. Therefore, singing a sweet song, she dips her hands in the water ans lets the water go in the wind, sprinkling it out of the trunk.

" Oh,what happens here, is it raining?" Violet, sitting on a park bench, raises her eyes up, feeling drops on her hair. No, no clouds in the sky: who knows, perhaps a passing bird peed upon her. Thus, she wipes her hair, disgusted. Again, she takes up her book, and begins the chapter, for the third time. It is strange: She always liked reading, or, better, she preferred it to other activities such as playing ball or hide-and-seek. But today she does not succeed in moving her eyes away from her school companions who are playing catch. They already asked to her to join them, and she, as usual, refused and took her book up. Then, of course they did not ask it again (on the contrary, at the beginning of the school year, they insisted on her playing with them). But, today, this fact makes her to feel alone. She, alone: a feeling that she had never felt before, because she always loved to stay alone. Now, each laughter, each cry makes her head raise from the book, and she loses the thread. She wonders how in the last days she could read without stopping , not caring of sounds and laughters, and.....*Toc, toc*...two drops fall on the page. Violet, again , raises her head looking up, where the sky is blue; at least, that part of the sky she sees through the tree branches. While looking up, a lot of drops fall down, all together, and wet her face, her eyes, her mouth...and, how strange, she seems also to hear a song...

Well, since here it is not possible to read in peace, perhaps this means that she ought to play with the others...She goes near the group, and , amazingly, hears herself asking: " Please, may I play with you?" Her humblity is rewarded by a hunanimous choir of "Yeeeeeah! You're the one which lasted to can play to five-corners, since finally we are five!"

And five are the petals falling from the tree, one by one, towards their path of transformation.

"Did you realize that his last was my own story? The flower I was devoted to taught me the virtue of Humility, the last virtue, but the first of the twelve steps towards God...

None of you could ever be alone, with God on her side, my dear little fairies...make a good job, and God bless you too!"

Yes, you can open your eyes, now.
I think you'd see better now, through the darkness, through the wood of the yew....Do you see Fairy Violet, and that little daisy fairy deeply asleep near her? Look, Fairy Violet sparkles some drops on her, whispering: "Rock Rose, Clematis, Impatiens...the rescue remedy to awaken the souls....Good awakening, dear...Would you like to grew up, now? You could begin your apprenticeship with a very easy task....Learn by heart the twelve stories, then fly over there, beyond the park gates..."
Close again your eyes, now...
Tomorrow morning you could think you did a strange dream, but inside you a light, musical, jingling voice will tell you twelve simple stories....

2007, Copyright Lulu editions

ISBN 978 – 1 – 84753 – 320 – 3

Printed in the United Kingdom
by Lightning Source UK Ltd.
126640UK00001BB/374/A